Dilys is looking after the café because Bella is ill. She's very busy, so she's asked someone to help her.

Norman is in a hurry. He's doing something important afterwards.

Before Norman leaves to play football, Dilys asks him to take a drink upstairs to Bella.

There's a noise at the door - who's that?

Rosa goes indoors for her food, and Dilys goes outside to hang out Bella's washing.

Norman calls down from the window.

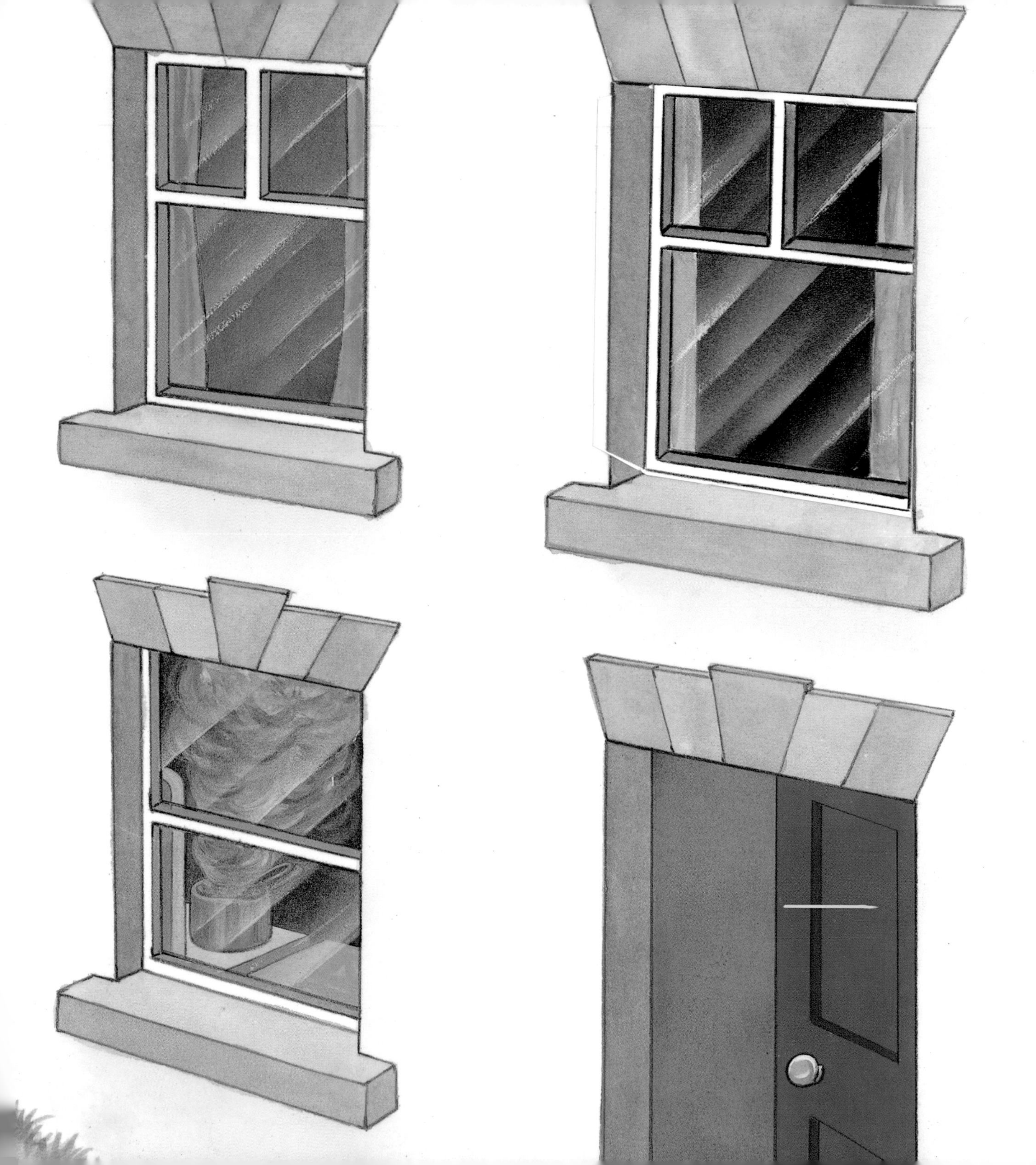

Norman can smell smoke from the kitchen. He and Bella rush outside and Norman telephones the fire brigade.

When the alarm rings, Fireman Sam, Elvis and Penny Morris know they must get to the café quickly.

When Jupiter arrives at the café, Bella is worried because Rosa is still in the kitchen. Fireman Sam and Penny choose the equipment they need.

Fireman Sam and Firefighter Penny Morris go into the kitchen to find Rosa.

Fireman Sam and Penny Morris put out the fire. Then Fireman Sam hears a noise coming from the cupboard.

The fire is out, everyone is safe, and Norman can go and play football at last!